The Pony-Mad Princess

Princess Ellie's Holiday Adventure

Ellie glanced at John. "Which way do
we go?" she asked.

There was a long pause while John
looked round thoughtfully. Then he
shrugged his shoulders and admitted,
"I don't know where we are. I think
we're lost."

GWASANAETH LLYFRGELL WRECSAM
WREXHAM LIBRARY SERVICE
Tynnwyd
o stoc
Withdrawn
from stock

D0493578

Look out for more sparkly adventures of

The Pony-Mad Princess!

The Pony-Mad Princess

Princess Ellie's Holiday Adventure

Diana Kimpton

Illustrated by Lizzie Finlay

WREXHAM C.B.C LIBRARY	
LLYFRGELL B.S. WRECSAM	
C56 0000 0536 367	
ASKEWS & HOLT	26-Apr-2012
JF	£4.99
JFIC	WR

First published in 2005 by Usborne Publishing Ltd., Usborne House,
83-85 Saffron Hill, London EC1N 8RT, England. www.usborne.com

Based on an original concept by Anne Finnis.

Text copyright © 2005 by Diana Kimpton and Anne Finnis.
Illustrations copyright © 2005 by Lizzie Finlay.
The right of Diana Kimpton and Anne Finnis to be identified as the authors
of this work and the right of Lizzie Finlay to be identified as the illustrator of
this work have been asserted by them in accordance with the Copyright,
Designs and Patents Act, 1988.

Cover photograph supplied by Sally Waters.

The name Usborne and the devices ♀ ⊕ are
Trade Marks of Usborne Publishing Ltd.

All rights reserved. No part of this publication may be reproduced,
stored in a retrieval system or transmitted in any form or by any means,
electronic, mechanical, photocopying, recording or otherwise without
the prior permission of the publisher.

This is a work of fiction. The characters, incidents, and dialogues are products
of the author's imagination and are not to be construed as real. Any resemblance
to actual events or persons, living or dead, is entirely coincidental.

A CIP catalogue record for this book is available from the British Library.

JFM MJJASOND/11   01429/1
ISBN 9780746067321
Printed in Chippenham, Eastbourne, UK.

Chapter 1

"Wow!" squealed Princess Ellie. "Look at those mountains."

"They're fantastic," agreed her best friend, Kate. "And they've got snow on the top."

"Of course they have," said Miss Stringle. "Andirovia is a much colder country than ours. Now do stop pressing your face against the car window, Princess Aurelia.

That's no way to behave. We can't have the public thinking princesses have squashed noses."

Ellie groaned as she sat back in her seat. She hated it when her governess called her by her real name. But she was too excited about the royal holiday to stay miserable for long. This was the first time she had ever visited Prince John and his family. She had never been to Andirovia before, and she'd never

seen mountains as big as these. She gazed longingly at the white peaks. "I've never seen real snow close up."

"I have," said Kate. "It's brilliant. Mum and Dad took me skiing once in the school holidays." Kate's parents

6

worked abroad and moved around a lot so she lived with her grandparents most of the time. Her gran was the palace cook.

"Let's ask if we can go up there and play snowballs," suggested Ellie.

"You'll ask no such thing," declared Miss Stringle. "You are guests and you must fit in with the activities arranged by your hosts."

Ellie hoped some of those plans would involve Prince John's ponies. The country they were driving through was perfect for riding. It was wild and free, with meadows,

forests and fast-flowing mountain streams. Andirovia really was as wonderful as John had described.

The car slowed down. It was the second in a line of gleaming black vehicles. Each one had a small Andirovian flag fluttering at the front. The first car held Ellie's parents, the King and Queen. The ones behind held their luggage and servants. To Ellie's disappointment, there was no horsebox. The King and Queen had insisted that all her ponies stayed at home.

She was already missing them. So she was delighted when she found the hold-up was caused by a lady riding a large, grey horse. The road was narrow here, so there wasn't room for the cars to overtake the rider safely. They had to drive slowly behind her until she turned into a gateway to let them through.

As her car swept past, Ellie gave the lady a royal wave, exactly as Miss Stringle had taught her in her waving lessons. "What a beautiful horse," she sighed.

"Where?" asked Kate, who'd been staring out of the opposite window. She turned round just in time to catch a glimpse of the grey and its rider before the car overtook them completely. Determined to see more, she swivelled round so she was kneeling on her seat. Then she watched them through the back window, waving wildly at the rider with both hands.

"Sit down at once," snapped Miss Stringle. "That is not how the public expect royalty to behave."

"But I'm not royal," said Kate.

Miss Stringle sighed. "I know that and so do you. But that woman doesn't."

Kate slowly turned round and faced the front again. She slumped miserably in her seat. "I'm never going to manage this," she groaned. "I don't know how to act royal."

Ellie smiled reassuringly. "It's easy enough. I do it."

"But you've had lots of lessons," said Kate. "I haven't. I'm going to let everyone down. I know I am."

Ellie was desperate to cheer Kate up. She knew her friend was nervous about coming on the royal holiday. But she had every right

to be there. She had
her own gold-edged
invitation from the
Emperor and Empress

of Andirovia. Prince John had insisted on it.

It was Miss Stringle who came to Kate's
rescue. "Don't worry, my dear," she said
kindly. "Just copy Princess Aurelia. She
knows what to do."

Ellie stared at her in surprise. Her
governess didn't usually have so much
confidence in her abilities.

At that moment, the cars rounded a bend
and Ellie saw Prince John's home for the first
time. "Wow!" she said for the second time
that day. John had been telling the truth.
His palace really was twice the size of the
one she lived in. It was built of white stone,

with strong towers at each corner like a castle.

"Look! There's a moat," cried Kate. "And swans."

"And a real drawbridge," added Ellie as the car whizzed across it and drew to a halt in the palace courtyard.

Princess Ellie's Holiday Adventure

The palace guard snapped to attention and the Emperor and Empress of Andirovia walked majestically down the front steps. Prince John was close behind, looking uncomfortable in his naval uniform. He peeped round his father and grinned at the girls.

A footman swung open the car door and a blast of cold air rushed inside. Ellie shivered and pulled her velvet cloak tight around her shoulders. Then she climbed out and led Kate over to join the King and Queen.

"How wonderful to see you," gushed the Empress. She kissed Ellie and Kate on the nose in the traditional Andirovian way. "Now come with us to inspect the palace guard."

"Oh dear," whispered Kate. "Is that hard?"

"No," replied Ellie. "We just walk along behind Mum and Dad and get bored."

The guardsmen looked bored, too, and very chilly. Their noses were red, their lips were blue and some of them were struggling to stop their teeth chattering. Ellie felt sorry for them. She felt sorry for herself as well and longed to get indoors. "It's freezing," she grumbled.

"No, it's not," declared John. "It's exactly 4° Celsius. Look – I've got this great new watch that tells the temperature as well as the time."

Ellie wasn't impressed. Cold weather would be fun if there was snow to play in. If there wasn't any, she much preferred to be warm. Perhaps Andirovia wasn't such a great place for a holiday after all.

Chapter 2

The inside of the palace was even more impressive than the outside. To Ellie's relief, it was also much warmer. A flurry of maids met them in the entrance hall with mugs of hot chocolate topped with whipped cream and marshmallows. Ellie sipped hers gratefully, wrapping her hands round it to thaw out her cold fingers.

She would have loved a second helping, but there wasn't time. The Emperor and Empress were keen to show off their home, so they whisked the visitors away on a conducted tour. Ellie loved the log fires that blazed in every room. The light from the flickering flames glittered on the swords and shields that hung on the walls.

By the time the girls were shown to their bedrooms, the maids had already unpacked their clothes. Ellie found it reassuring to see her own dressing gown hanging on the back of the door and her pink alarm clock on the bedside table. They helped her feel less homesick.

Princess Ellie's Holiday Adventure

She opened the small suitcase on the bed – the one she'd told the maid not to touch. Inside were her riding clothes. She buried her face in them, breathing in the welcome smell of horse. Then she put them neatly on a chair, plonked her riding hat on top and went back to the case.

At the bottom, were five rectangular packages. Ellie took them out one by one and carefully unwrapped their tissue paper covering. Inside each one was a framed photograph of one of her ponies – Shadow, Sundance, Moonbeam, Rainbow and Starlight.

Ellie sighed. She already missed them so much. But at least the photos made them feel less far away. She arranged them on top of a chest of drawers, so she could see them easily when she was in bed. Then she carefully moved the photo of Shadow so it was next to the one of Sundance – the two ponies were good friends and always stood next to each other in their field.

As she stood back to admire her work, Kate bounded through the door. "My room's fantastic," she shrieked. "I've got a four-poster bed and it's really bouncy." She paused and looked at the photographs.

Princess Ellie's Holiday Adventure

"Great. You've brought pictures, too. That gives me an idea."

She rushed out and came back clutching a framed photo of a skewbald foal. She put it down carefully beside Ellie's picture of Starlight. "That's better. Now my Angel's with her mum and all the ponies are together."

"Boo!" said John, who'd crept up behind them when they weren't looking. He laughed when they both jumped. Then he looked at the pictures and said, "Hasn't Angel grown?" He hadn't seen the foal since the day she was born – the same day Ellie gave her to Kate.

"She's clever, too," said Kate, proudly. "She's learned to wear a headcollar and she lifts up her feet so I can clean them with a hoof pick."

"Can you ride her yet?" asked John.

Kate laughed. "Of course not. She's still only a baby. She won't be strong enough to carry me until she's three or four."

"But that doesn't matter," said Ellie. "Kate can ride my ponies while she's waiting. And talking of ponies – when can we see yours?"

John grinned. "How about now?"

Kate looked doubtful. "Miss Stringle said we've got to get ready for the banquet soon."

"There's loads of time for that," said John. "Come on. Follow me."

He led them down a long corridor. It was dark and gloomy. The wood-panelled walls were covered with paintings of old-fashioned people and stags on mountain tops.

At the far end was a long, curving staircase. But just as they were about to go down, they spotted Miss Stringle at the bottom.

"Oh, no!" groaned Ellie. "I bet she's looking for us."

"Then let's make sure she doesn't find you," laughed John. "It's time I showed you our secret passage." He ran back down the corridor and pressed hard on one of the panels. A hidden door creaked slowly open. "Quick. In here."

The two girls ran towards him. Behind her, Ellie could hear Miss Stringle's footsteps growing louder and louder as she neared the top of the stairs. Soon, the governess would step into the corridor and see them both. Then she was sure to take them back to their rooms to get ready. There wouldn't be another chance to see John's ponies today.

The secret passage was the only way to escape. But Ellie and Kate both hesitated when they reached the hidden door. It looked very dark and scary on the other side.

Chapter 3

Ellie plucked up her courage and stepped through the secret doorway. Then she grabbed Kate's hand and pulled her friend after her. John followed swiftly and pulled the door closed behind him.

They huddled together in the darkness, hardly daring to breathe while they listened to Miss Stringle's footsteps grow closer and closer. Ellie was sure her governess would stop when she reached the door, but she didn't. She marched straight on without even hesitating.

"She never guessed we were here," squealed Ellie, after the footsteps had disappeared into the distance.

"Where is here, anyway?" asked Kate.

"I'll show you," said John and he clicked on a torch.

"Where did you get that from?" asked Kate.

"I leave it here just in case," explained John. "A good explorer can never be sure when he'll need to use a secret passage." He was almost as keen on exploring as he was on ponies.

Ellie looked round. They were in a narrow

tunnel built with brick. "Where does it go?" she asked.

"Outside," said John. "If we go to the stables this way, there's no chance of us bumping into Miss Stringle again."

He led the way along the passage and down a twisting, spiral staircase with uneven, stone steps. It was very steep and very narrow. Ellie was glad when she reached the bottom and John swung open a heavy door.

As soon as she stepped outside, she wished she'd brought her coat with her.

It was colder than ever. She was fascinated to see her breath hang like a cloud on the still air.

She stood shivering with Kate, while John closed the door. On this side, it was disguised to look like stone. It blended perfectly with the wall. No one would find it unless they already knew it was there.

As soon as he'd finished, John led them quickly round the side of the palace to the stables. Ellie was surprised to find they were quite different from hers at home. Those were arranged around an open courtyard, so each of her ponies had a door to the outside. John's were tucked inside a cosy barn. A wide passage ran down the middle. On one side was a tack room, a feed store and a huge pile of hay and straw. On the

other was a line of four stables, but only two
of them were occupied.

"This one's
Toffee, and this
one's Fudge,"
said John,
pointing to each
of his chestnut
ponies in turn.

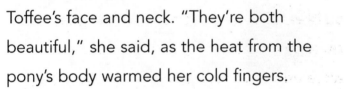

Ellie stroked
Toffee's face and neck. "They're both
beautiful," she said, as the heat from the
pony's body warmed her cold fingers.

"They're like twins," laughed Kate.
"How do you tell which is which?"

"That's easy," explained John. "Toffee
has a tiny white mark on her nose."

It was so small that Ellie had to look

carefully before she spotted it. "I wish I could try riding her."

"There isn't time," said Kate.

"And it's nearly dark," added John.

Ellie tried not to feel too disappointed. "Never mind," she said. "We can still play with them for a bit." She divided Toffee's mane into sections and started to twist the hairs into neat plaits.

Before she'd finished the first one, the barn door swung open. Miss Stringle marched in, and this time there was nowhere to hide.

Princess Ellie's Holiday Adventure

"I've been looking for you everywhere," grumbled the governess. "It's very late. You should be getting ready for the banquet." She seized the girls by their hands and led them unwillingly towards the door.

"We'll all go for a ride tomorrow," called John.

"We can't," said Kate. "There's three of us and only two ponies."

"Bother," said Ellie. They couldn't leave one person behind – that would be so unfair. And it wouldn't be fun if they couldn't all go together. But she hadn't been on a pony since she left home, and she couldn't bear the thought of not riding for the whole week she was here. There must be *something* they could do.

Chapter 4

Miss Stringle marched the girls to their rooms. Then she waited impatiently while they bathed in sweet-smelling pink bubbles and changed into their evening clothes.

Soon, Ellie was dressed in a pink silk ball gown. It had flouncy sleeves and the skirt was embroidered with golden horseshoes. Her sandals were gold, too, and so was her tiara. Miss Stringle inspected her carefully, straightened the hem of her dress and patted her curls into place.

She had just finished when Kate stepped nervously into the room. "Do I look all right?" she asked. "Gran made this for me specially." The dress was pale blue and the material shimmered as she moved.

"You look great," said Ellie. She had never seen her friend look so pretty before.

But Miss Stringle seemed less sure. "It just needs a little something more." She pulled a large bunch of ribbons from her bag, selected two silver ones and gently tied them in Kate's hair.

Kate looked at herself in the mirror and smiled. "Thank you. They look perfect."

"Of course they do," said Miss Stringle with a smile. Then she switched to a more matter-of-fact voice and continued, "Now come along with me and remember your manners. Sit up straight. Do not stick spoons on your noses. Do not play tunes on the drinking glasses. Only use the round spoon for soup…"

The list went on and on. It lasted all the way to the banquet. As they followed the King and Queen through the

door, Kate whispered, "I'll never remember
all that."

"You'll be fine," Ellie whispered back.
"Just copy me."

The banqueting hall looked beautiful.
The tables were covered with snow-white
cloths, and decorated with
bowls of red roses
and swans carved
out of ice. The
knives and forks were
made of gold and so were the candlesticks.
Ellie loved the gentle glow of the candles,
which made everything sparkle and shine.

Ellie was pleased to find that she and
Kate were sitting next to John. She was less
pleased when the butler ladled soup into
her china bowl. It was a strange green

colour and smelled of fish. But, at least, it was easy to spot the soup spoon amongst the huge selection of cutlery in front of her. She picked it up very slowly and waited until she was sure Kate had copied her. Then she pushed her sleeves out of the way and started to eat.

The soup was even worse than it looked. It was flavoured with chilli and tasted hotter than any curry Ellie had ever eaten. She swallowed it as quickly as possible. But, by the time she had finished, her tongue felt as if it was on fire. Desperate to cool her mouth, she gulped down the entire contents of her glass of lemonade. Out of the corner of her eye, she noticed Kate do the same.

A maid whisked away the empty bowl and replaced it with a gold-rimmed plate.

Then the butler placed something small, black and crispy in the middle of it.

Ellie eyed the lump of food suspiciously. There was something vaguely familiar about its shape, but she couldn't quite place what it was. "It looks disgusting," she whispered.

"It is," said John. "But I'm afraid it's a traditional dish to serve to visitors."

Ellie wondered whether to cut the object into little bits or eat it all at once. Then she made up her mind, stabbed it with her fork and popped the whole thing in her mouth.

Kate was more cautious. She examined the black lump on the end of her fork and asked, "What's it called?"

"Andirovian Slug Surprise," announced John.

Ellie nearly choked. She longed to spit

the slug out, but she knew she mustn't. That would be much too rude. Now it was in her mouth, she had to eat it. She summoned all her courage and forced herself to bite it in half. As soon as her teeth broke the crisp outer shell, thick goo trickled out. It was bitter and disgusting.

Ellie swallowed as hard as she could.

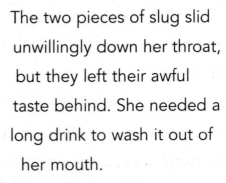

The two pieces of slug slid unwillingly down her throat, but they left their awful taste behind. She needed a long drink to wash it out of her mouth.

But her glass was empty. She'd already drunk all the lemonade to cool her tongue after the soup. Ellie looked desperately round the table. The taste of slug was unbearable. There must be something else she could drink.

She lunged forward and grabbed the water jug. But, in her haste, she forgot about the flouncy sleeve of her ball gown, which knocked over two glasses, a salt pot and a flask of vinegar. They rolled away and knocked down other glasses. Those, in turn, knocked down even more. The disaster spread down the long table like a row of tumbling dominoes. Stains spread across the once-white cloth and guests leaped to their feet to avoid the spilled wine.

Kate put her hand across her mouth to stop herself giggling. "Shall I copy you?" she asked.

A small part of Ellie wanted to laugh too. But the rest of her didn't. She'd ruined the meal and knew she was in big trouble. But, now she was in Andirovia, she didn't know what sort of trouble that would be. Perhaps she'd be grounded like the children she'd read about in her pony books. Then there'd be no fun, no snowballs and, worst of all, no riding.

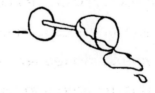

Chapter 5

Ellie found it hard to sleep that night.
To her surprise, the Emperor and Empress
had been very kind about her accident.
They'd ordered the maids to clear up the
mess and never mentioned any type of
punishment. But the King and Queen had
glowered at her angrily and Miss Stringle
had threatened her with extra lessons on

table manners when they got home.

Worse still, she was cold. The roaring log fire had died down to a dull glow that gave out little heat. Cold draughts blew through the gaps in the windows and made her shiver. She wished she was back at home in her bedroom. For once, she didn't mind that it was much too pink. She just wanted to be cuddled up under her favourite quilt – the one decorated with pictures of ponies.

At last, she decided there was no point in tossing and turning any longer. She snuggled right under the heavy blankets, switched on her torch and started to read her book. The picture on the cover made her feel homesick – it was a palomino pony just like Moonbeam. In the story, it belonged to two children who faced exactly

the same problem as Ellie and her friends –
they couldn't go out for a ride together. But
they had found a solution. It was a bicycle.
"That would work for us, too," thought Ellie,
just before she finally fell asleep. "I hope
John's got one."

"Of course I have," declared John at
breakfast time. "It's the best mountain bike
in Andirovia, and it's red."

"Is that important?" asked Kate.

"Who cares," said Ellie. She gulped down
the last of her toast and leaped to her feet.
"Come on!" she yelled. Then she
remembered her manners. She sat down
again, folded her napkin neatly and asked,
"Please may we leave the table?"

"We're all going riding," explained John.

"No, you're not," said the Emperor.

"The ponies will have to wait until this afternoon," said the King. "We're being taken on an outing this morning."

"To see our new ice-cream factory," explained the Empress, with an enthusiastic smile. "I'm sure you'll find it fascinating."

Ellie didn't. She liked ice cream. But she found it difficult to get excited about shiny pipes and big vats of gloop. She didn't even enjoy the tasting session. The weather in Andirovia was so chilly that she wondered why anyone here wanted to eat cold food. Hot syrup sponge and custard sounded much more appealing.

The morning dragged slowly by. So did the long, boring lunch with the local mayor. But eventually the meal was over and they could finally go for their ride. Ellie and Kate were determined not to let the cold weather ruin their afternoon, so they dressed as cosily as they could. They put thick

fleeces under their wax jackets, two pairs of socks inside their riding boots and warm riding gloves on their hands.

John was waiting for them outside the barn with

Toffee and Fudge. They were already saddled and bridled. "I asked Ivan, the groom, to tack them up," he explained. "I didn't want to waste any more riding time."

"Who's going on the bike first?" asked Kate.

"I will," said John. "It is mine, after all."

"Can I have Toffee then?" asked Ellie. "She's the one I wanted to ride yesterday."

John laughed. "Only if you can tell which one she is."

Ellie inspected the two ponies carefully and soon spotted the telltale white mark on Toffee's nose. "This one," she announced, as she took the pony's reins. Then she checked the girth was tight enough and swung herself into the saddle. Kate followed her lead and mounted Fudge.

John proudly fetched his gleaming red mountain bike from the barn. "It's got twenty-four gears, alloy wheels and a top-of-the-range computer."

"What good's a computer on a bike?" asked Kate.

John looked at her as if she was a complete fool. "It tells you your current speed, your average speed, your maximum speed, how far you've gone, how many times you've turned the pedals and…"

"Okay, that's enough," said Kate. "I believe you."

"And it's got a stopwatch to time when we have to change over," John continued, completely ignoring her interruption.

"That does sound useful," said Ellie.

"Of course it is," said John. He leaned forward and pressed a button on the computer. "Now let's get going."

It was wonderful to be riding again. Toffee and Fudge obviously thought so too. They walked forward willingly with their ears pricked and their necks arched.

"Which way shall we go?" asked Ellie, as they clattered across the drawbridge. "Can we go up to where the snow is?"

John laughed and shook his head. "It's much further away than it looks. We'll explore the pine forest instead. The paths there will be good for the bike."

Soon they were deep in the forest, trotting between the tall trees. Ellie was enjoying herself despite her disappointment about the snow. She felt warmer now she was on the move and she loved the smell of the crisp, cold air. It was very different from home, and very quiet. The ground was covered with a thick layer of pine needles, so the ponies' feet hardly made a sound.

After a while, the silence was broken by a loud bleeping. "Changeover time," called John, as he reset the computer. "It's your turn to cycle, Ellie."

As soon as they'd swapped over, Ellie

discovered John's bike was harder to ride than she'd expected. The pine needles on the path made pedalling hard work. The gears didn't help much, either. There were so many of them that she didn't know which one to use.

She was soon out of breath, but she didn't complain. The bike had been her idea in the first place, and she was determined to

keep up. Then John and Kate pushed the ponies into a canter. Ellie tried to pedal faster, but her legs were too tired. Soon Toffee and Fudge were well ahead, their hooves flying along the path as it curved round the edge of a clearing.

Ellie was about to admit defeat when she spotted a way to catch up. If she cut straight across the middle of the clearing, she would reach the other side at the same time as the ponies.

She rode off the path as fast as she could and headed for the other side. But the ground was much bumpier than it looked and the bushes had long thorns that tore at her clothes.

"Be careful," yelled John, but it was too late. A dead branch caught in the front wheel. The bike stopped instantly, and Ellie sailed over the handlebars.

Luckily, only her pride was hurt. She clambered to her feet just as the others trotted over.

"Thank goodness you're all right," said Kate.

"What about my bike?" asked John.

Ellie pulled it upright and checked it carefully. The red paint still gleamed. The wheels still went round and the computer was still ticking away the minutes until the next changeover. But there was a long thorn sticking out of the front wheel. The tyre was completely flat.

Chapter 6

"I'm sorry," said Ellie, as she pulled the thorn out of the tyre. The last of the air escaped with a gentle hiss.

"Can the computer mend punctures?" teased Kate.

"Of course not," said John. "But I can. I've got the best puncture repair kit in the country. It's got explorer-grade super-sticky glue, extra-strong patches and an electronic gadget to measure the tyre pressure." His confident smile faded as he reached into each of his pockets in turn. Then his ears turned pink with embarrassment. "I've left it at home," he admitted, in a quiet voice.

"It's all my fault," said Ellie. "You two go on and enjoy your ride. I'll meet you at the stables." She picked up the bike and started to push it back the way they'd come.

"That's not fair," said Kate. "It could have happened to any of us, and it won't be so much fun without you."

"Kate's right," agreed John. "And you

might get lost on your own. We'll all go home together."

They turned the ponies round and headed back to the palace. Luckily, John knew a short cut, so they reached the stables sooner than Ellie expected.

"It's a pity it all went wrong," she said, as she pushed the bike into the barn. Then she stopped and stared in surprise. The barn wasn't empty. In the stable at the far end stood the biggest horse she had ever seen. "Who's that?" she asked.

"He's called Goliath," answered John. "He belongs to Ivan, the groom. I'll introduce you as soon as we've tied up Toffee and Fudge."

The horse looked even bigger close up. He was jet black, with a huge head, strong

neck and enormous hooves. But he seemed very gentle. He pricked his ears forward happily when Ellie reached up to stroke his face. Then he rubbed his head against her shoulder and nearly knocked her over.

"I don't understand," said Kate. "Why didn't we see him yesterday?"

"Because he wasn't here," John explained. "He only came back this morning. Ivan's brother had borrowed him. He loves riding, but he hasn't got a horse of his own."

"I know how he feels," said Kate. She

had longed for a pony for years before Ellie gave her Angel.

"It's a shame Goliath's not a pony," said Ellie. "If he was, we could borrow him and all go riding together."

John's eyes lit up with excitement. "Let's do it anyway. I'm a brilliant rider. I'm sure I can manage him."

"I'm not," said Kate, with a worried expression on her face.

"Neither am I," agreed Ellie. "He's much too big for you."

"No, he's not!" John insisted. He straightened his back to make himself look as tall as possible. "Anyway, size doesn't matter. Jockeys are short and they ride big horses."

Ellie knew that was true. But it didn't

calm her fears. She suspected even a racehorse would look small beside Goliath. He looked strong enough to carry a knight in full armour. "Perhaps we should ask Ivan," she suggested.

"We can't," said John. "He's not here and we won't have time to ride if we go looking for him."

"But suppose he comes back before we do," said Kate. "He'll think someone has stolen Goliath."

"Not if we leave a note," answered John. He led the way to the tack room to fetch Goliath's saddle and bridle.

Putting the bridle on was easier than any of them expected. The gentle horse lowered his head for them to reach and opened his mouth so they could slip the metal bit between his teeth. Putting on the saddle was a much harder task. It was big and heavy and Goliath's back was a long way up. None of them could lift the saddle high enough.

"I wish he'd kneel down like a camel," said Kate. "Then we'd be able to reach."

Ellie ran to the tack room and came back carrying a battered, wooden chair. "If we can't make him shorter, we'll have to make us taller. Hold his head, both of you. Make sure he doesn't move."

She picked up the saddle, moved the chair as close as she could to Goliath and climbed onto it. The extra height made all the difference. She managed to place the saddle gently on the horse's back. She was careful to put it slightly in front of where it should go. Then she slid it back into the right position to make sure all the hairs on his back were lying flat.

She fastened the girth that held the saddle in place. Then she jumped down and carried the chair outside. "You'll need this," she told John. "You'll never get on him without it."

Kate followed her with Goliath, while John paused for a moment to fasten the note to the stable door.

The huge, black horse really was a gentle giant.

He had stood patiently while they struggled to put on his saddle. Now he stood completely still again while John clambered on board from the chair. But as soon as he felt his rider's weight on his back, Goliath was eager to be on the move. He stamped his feet restlessly while John shortened the stirrups.

Kate held the horse's head to stop him walking away. She looked at John and giggled. "You look tiny up there. Like a pimple on a mountain."

John ignored her comments. He shortened the reins and announced, "You can let go now. I'm in control."

Kate did as she was told and ran into the barn with Ellie to fetch the ponies. When they led them outside, they found Goliath walking round and round in small circles.

"Are you all right?" asked Ellie.

"Of course, I am," said John. But his voice sounded less confident than it had earlier. "He's just restless. That's all. He'll be fine when we get on the move."

This time it was Ellie's turn to ride Fudge while Kate took Toffee. John continued to ride in circles while they mounted. Then he let the big horse lead the way across the drawbridge and out into the grounds.

Goliath didn't want to walk. He kept snorting through his enormous nostrils and trying to go faster. "Steady, boy," pleaded John, struggling to keep the horse under control. He sat down firmly in the saddle and kept a tight hold on the reins.

As they left the shelter of the palace,

Princess Ellie's Holiday Adventure

Ellie noticed for the first time that the weather had changed. Thick clouds had blown in from the north, covering the sky with a heavy, grey blanket and hiding the tops of the mountains. A chill wind stung their cheeks and lifted the ponies' manes. It seemed to make Goliath even more restless.

"Perhaps we should have a trot," said Ellie. "A good long trot would use up some of his energy."

John nodded nervously. He lengthened the reins a little and Goliath started to jog. The huge horse was very excited now. He tossed his head from side to side and snorted again. Then he dropped his head down towards his knees.

The movement happened so suddenly that John was nearly pulled over Goliath's shoulder. To save himself, he had to let the reins slip through his fingers. The enormous horse immediately noticed what had happened. Realizing his rider had lost control, Goliath threw his head up again and bolted into the distance.

Chapter 7

Ellie and Kate watched in horror as Goliath galloped away across an open stretch of grass. His huge hooves thundered on the ground.

"Stop him!" yelled Kate.

"I can't," wailed John. He'd caught hold of the reins again and was pulling on them as hard as he could. But Goliath was too strong for him. He didn't want to obey his rider. He was enjoying himself too much.

"We've got to follow them," said Ellie, squeezing her legs against Fudge's sides. The chestnut pony did as she was told. She started to canter and then to gallop, racing after Goliath, with Toffee and Kate at her side.

Ellie crouched low over Fudge's neck, urging the pony to go faster and faster. Normally, she loved galloping. But today she was too scared to enjoy it. She just concentrated on following Goliath. He'd reached the end of the open grassland, now, and hurtled into a wooded area. But he didn't slow down. He raced on at full speed, twisting and turning between the trees.

Princess Ellie's Holiday Adventure

The ponies rushed after him. Their manes and tails streamed behind them in the wind as they galloped on and on, further and further from the palace. The race seemed to be going on for ever. Ellie couldn't remember the last time she had galloped so far.

But Goliath's legs were so long that he could cover the ground much faster than Toffee and Fudge. There was no way they

could keep up with the huge horse.
Although Ellie and Kate urged them on as
fast as they could, the two ponies were
gradually left behind.

Ellie kept her eyes on Goliath. She hoped
desperately that John would stay in the
saddle and not fall off. But it became harder
and harder to keep the huge horse in sight
as the gap between them grew. Eventually,
Goliath galloped behind a clump of trees
and disappeared from sight.

"Oh, no!" groaned Kate. "We've lost
them."

Ellie's stomach knotted with fear, but she
tried to stay calm. There was nothing to be
gained by panicking now. "We'll find him.
I'm sure we will," she said, as much to
convince herself as her friend.

"We've got to," said Kate. "We can't leave him out here on his own."

"And we need him to show us the way back," added Ellie. They had zigzagged so much during that long gallop that she'd completely lost her sense of direction.

Toffee and Fudge were tired now. They had done their best, but they were puffing hard and wanted to slow down. Ellie knew it wasn't fair to push them any harder. "We'd better let them rest," she said.

The ponies seemed happy to stop. They stood with their heads down and their sides heaving, as they struggled to get their breath back. Their necks were soaked with sweat despite the cold weather.

"Goliath must be tired, too," said Kate. "Perhaps he'll stop as well."

"I hope so," said Ellie, turning up the collar of her coat to protect herself from the cold wind. "Let's go and look. We need to keep the ponies moving or they'll get chilled."

She pushed Fudge into a walk, leaving her reins long so the pony could stretch her neck. Kate did the same with Toffee and, side by side, they rode over to the last place they'd seen John and Goliath.

"John!" shouted Ellie.

There was no reply.

"Can you hear us?" yelled Kate.

Still nothing.

"We'll have to go on a bit further," said Ellie. She rode

Fudge to the next clump of trees and called again. "Where are you?"

This time there was an answering shout. "I'm over here," came the faint reply.

The girls shortened their ponies' reins and trotted off in the direction of the sound. To their delight, they soon found Goliath again, with John still on his back. The huge horse had calmed down now. He was eating the grass as if nothing had ever gone wrong.

John looked less happy. "That was exciting," he said, smiling weakly.

"That was terrifying," corrected Kate.

Ellie nodded in agreement. Then she giggled. "It's a good thing you didn't fall off. We'd never have got you back on without that chair."

John laughed. "That's why I didn't get off while I was waiting for you."

"Had we better get going?" said Kate. "We galloped for ages. It's going to be a long ride back."

Ellie glanced at John. "Which way do we go?" she asked.

There was a long pause while John looked round thoughtfully. Then, he shrugged his shoulders and admitted, "I don't know where we are. I think we're lost."

Chapter 8

Ellie stared at John in disbelief. "You must know where we are. You live here."

"Our palace grounds are much larger than yours," declared John, in his best superior voice. "I haven't managed to explore them all yet."

"Surely you can see somewhere you recognize," said Kate. "How about that

strange-shaped tree
over there? The one
that's bent over like
an old man with a
walking stick."

John shook
his head.
"I've never
seen it before. Anyway, trees aren't a good
way of finding out where you are. Real
explorers use the sun and the stars and the
mountain tops to guide them."

"Go on, then," said Ellie. "You're always
saying how you want to be an explorer."

They all looked up at the sky. The clouds
that filled it looked even darker than they
had earlier. They were lower, too. They
didn't just hide the peaks of the mountains.

Now they reached halfway down their slopes.

"So much for that idea," said Kate. "No sun, no stars and no mountain tops. What does a real explorer do at a time like this?"

John thought for a moment. Then he grinned triumphantly. "It's simple. We just follow our tracks back the way we've come. I've got this brilliant survival guide at home. It's taught me all about tracking."

He pulled Goliath's head up, shortened the reins and walked him round in a circle. As he rode, John stared intently at the ground. Then he pointed to a large hoof print. "See that? That means Goliath and I must have come that way."

Ellie was impressed. The hoof print was quite faint. She would never have spotted it.

"Here's another one," called John. "And there's a freshly snapped twig. Goliath must have trodden on it."

Kate and Ellie joined in the search. It was fun – like a treasure hunt. Each new sign was a fresh clue showing them the way back to the palace. Their progress was slow because they had to look so carefully. But they were sure they would get back in the end.

A tiny speck of white floated down from the sky and landed on Fudge's mane. It lay there for a moment. Then it melted and disappeared. Soon another one fell and then another. Ellie felt a thrill of excitement as she realized what they were. "It's snowing," she cried. She looked up at the sky, letting the tiny flakes fall on her face.

"Fantastic," yelled Kate. "I love snow." She poked out her tongue and tried to catch the flakes with it.

John and Ellie did the same. Soon, all three of them were so absorbed in their new game that they completely forgot their hunt for tracks. The flakes were bigger now and there were more of them. They didn't melt when they landed. Instead, they stayed on the ground, covering it with a carpet of white.

Ellie rode up to a tree and ran her hand along a branch, picking up the snow that had settled there. "I've got a snowball," she sang, holding it above her head as if she was about to throw it at John.

"Don't!" he pleaded. "If you hit Goliath, he might bolt again."

Ellie grinned. "I was only teasing." She threw the ball at the tree instead. It hit the trunk with a satisfying thud and smashed to

pieces. She'd started a new game. Soon, they were all making snowballs and tossing them at the trees.

Kate was the first to tire of it. "I'm getting hungry," she said. "Let's go back."

Ellie looked round. The world looked completely different now. The ground was covered with a smooth blanket of pure, white snow. It hid the earth, the grass and the fallen twigs.

To her horror, Ellie realized it also hid all the tracks they had been following. It was impossible to find them now. And without those tracks they couldn't find their way home.

Chapter 9

Ellie bit her lip nervously. "What shall we do now?"

"Panic?" suggested Kate.

"Don't be silly," said John. "Explorers never panic." He pointed through the falling snow. "I'm sure we came from over there."

Ellie nodded. Far off in the distance, she could faintly see the strange shape of the tree Kate had pointed out. "Does that help?" she asked.

"Of course it does," said John. "If we know where we were and we know where we are now, we can work out the direction we've been travelling in. So if we keep going the same way, we'll get home."

"I hope so," said Kate, with a shiver. "My gloves are wet from making snowballs and my fingers are cold."

"Me too," agreed Ellie. She wasn't completely sure she understood John's plan, but she was willing to give it a try. "Let's get moving. It's freezing."

"You're right," said John, checking the thermometer on his watch. "It's exactly zero degrees. Brrr, freezing." Then he shortened his reins and announced, "I'll go in front.

I'm the most experienced at exploring, so I'm sure to be the best at finding our way."
He made Goliath walk forward and set off slowly, looking back occasionally to check the direction.

Ellie let Kate and Toffee go next. She and Fudge went last in line. The snow didn't seem as exciting now. There was already so much of it and it was still falling.

As they rode on, the weather got even worse. The snow fell faster and faster. The wind grew stronger too, whipping the flakes into their faces to sting their cold cheeks. They rode hunched up against the cold, with their heads down to get some protection from the brims of their hats.

Soon they were riding through a whirling world of white. Ellie glanced back to see if they were still travelling in a straight line. But the falling flakes covered their hoof prints so quickly that it wasn't possible to tell any more. "Are you sure we're going the right way?" she shouted.

"Of course, I am," John called back. "Trust me. I know what I'm doing."

It was snowing even harder now. The

flakes were so close together that it was hard to see between them. Ellie felt as if she was surrounded by a wall of white. She urged Fudge to walk faster to make sure she kept close to the others. She didn't want to get separated from them in this blizzard.

At first, the pony seemed happy to obey. She trudged through the snow, following behind Toffee without Ellie having to do much to guide her. But then she started to be awkward. First she tried to turn to the right. Then she tried to turn to the left. Then she tried to whirl round and go the other way.

"Please stop it," begged Ellie. The ride was already bad enough. Now it was turning into a battle of wills between her

and the chestnut pony. She was determined
to win. It was bad enough being lost with
John and Kate. It would be dreadful to be
out here in the snow on her own.

She kept her reins short and her legs
close to Fudge's sides. Every time the pony
started to dart away, Ellie managed to stop
her. But it was hard work. Soon she was
sweating inside her jacket despite the cold
weather.

Kate turned round and noticed Fudge's
behaviour. "What's wrong?" she asked.

"She won't do as she's told," wailed Ellie.
"She doesn't want to follow you. She wants
to go off on her own."

"That's weird," called John from the
front. "She's usually very well behaved."

"Perhaps it's because of the weather,"

suggested Kate. "It's a bit scary when you can't see anything except snow!"

Ellie felt better, knowing there was a possible explanation. Then the snow started to ease. With fewer flakes falling, they could see much further through the white wilderness that surrounded them. But Fudge's behaviour didn't improve. Something else must be wrong.

"Look," said Kate. "There's another one of those strange-shaped trees."

Ellie stared at it. It looked exactly like an old man with a walking stick. "How peculiar," she said. "You wouldn't expect to have two trees like that so close together."

Then she had a dreadful thought. "You don't think...?" Her voice died away.

She didn't want to say it out loud.

But John did it for her. "It's the same tree," he sighed. "We've gone round in a circle."

Chapter 10

Goliath and Toffee stood quietly beside the strange tree with their heads down. They looked as tired and miserable as their riders. Snow covered their manes and frosted their ears. But Fudge was still restless. She kept stamping her feet and trying to walk away.

Ellie felt a rising tide of panic as she struggled to make the pony stand still. They really were completely lost. "What are we going to do?" she asked.

"I'm not sure yet," replied John. "There's no point in following our tracks again. They'll only bring us back here."

"We can't see them anyway," said Kate. "The snow's already covered them up." She looked round nervously and added, "It'll start getting dark soon."

Ellie shivered, partly from cold and partly from fear. "We'll freeze if we're out here all night."

"No, we won't," said John. "We can build an igloo. I've read all about how to do it in my survival guide. You just cut big chunks of snow and..."

"Stop it!" yelled Kate. "I don't want to do that. I want to go home."

"So do I," said Ellie. "There might be wolves."

"Not many," said John, brightly. "The Andirovian silver-backed wolf is an endangered species."

That was more than Kate could cope with. "I'm scared," she cried. "I'm tired and I'm cold and I'm very, very hungry."

"I expect the ponies are, too," said Ellie, suddenly aware of her own empty stomach.

"Maybe that's what's wrong with Fudge," suggested John. "She's much greedier than Toffee. When I take her out on a ride, she's always in a hurry to get back for her feed."

Princess Ellie's Holiday Adventure

His words gave Ellie a glimmer of hope. "Do you mean she's one of those ponies that always seems to know when you've turned for home?"

"Definitely," said John. "She always speeds up then."

A slow smile spread across Ellie's face. "If she's trying to go home now, that might mean she knows the way."

"Or it might not," said Kate, gloomily.

"But it's worth a try," said Ellie. "We've got nothing to lose."

"And we can always build an igloo later," added John.

Ellie ignored him. She let the reins slip through her fingers until they hung so loosely that Fudge was free to go in whichever direction she pleased. Then Ellie squeezed her legs against the pony's sides. "Go on, girl. Take us home."

Fudge didn't need any more encouragement. She turned and walked away from the strange-looking tree in a very determined fashion. The others followed her, their hooves crunching on the snow.

Sometimes, Fudge led them between trees whose branches sagged under the weight of their white covering. Sometimes, she plunged through snowdrifts that reached her knees. But she never hesitated. She really seemed to know where she was going.

At long last, they rode out from a patch of pine trees and saw the palace straight ahead of them. Fudge whinnied in triumph and found a new store of energy. She started to trot and then to canter. Goliath and Toffee did the same. Soon, all three of them were racing towards the safety of home.

Now the ride was nearly over, Ellie was beginning to enjoy it again. She glanced at John and Kate and saw they were smiling, too.

They slowed the horses as they reached the moat, trotted sedately over the drawbridge and came to a halt in the courtyard.

As they swung themselves wearily out of their saddles, two footmen unrolled a long, red carpet down the snow-covered steps. The Emperor and Empress raced down it, closely followed by the King and Queen.

"We've been so worried about you," wailed the Empress. She hugged John dramatically, pulling his face so close to her chest that he could hardly breathe.

"We were about to send out a search party," said the Queen, dabbing her eyes with a lace-trimmed handkerchief.

The Emperor looked at John sternly. "Ivan was worried you might have had problems with Goliath."

"Oh, no," replied John, as he struggled free of his mother's arms. "He's had a lovely time."

Ellie knew that wasn't a lie, but it wasn't the whole truth, either. John obviously didn't want to admit what really happened, but he might have to if they kept questioning him. Somehow, they had to change the subject.

"Fudge was the real hero," she cried, throwing her arms around the chestnut pony's neck. "She brought us safely back."

Her plan worked. The adults were so keen to learn more about Fudge's cleverness that they didn't ask any more awkward questions about Goliath.

"You'd better come inside and get warm,"

said the Emperor, when the explanations were over. "Ivan can look after the horses."

"But we'll help," said John. "All real explorers look after their ponies before they look after themselves."

They led Toffee, Fudge and Goliath back to the barn. Ivan had already put a thick layer of clean straw on the floor of each stable and hung up nets bulging with sweet-smelling hay.

Just as they finished taking off the saddles and bridles, a maid arrived carrying three large mugs of drinking chocolate on a gold tray. Ellie sipped hers happily, feeling the hot liquid warm her from the inside. "I think I've had enough of snow for today," she said.

"And enough of exploring," said Kate.

"Perhaps tomorrow we should stay closer to home," suggested John. Then he grinned and added, "We could build that igloo."

"Snowmen would be more fun," said Kate.

"I've got an even better idea," said Ellie. "Let's make snow ponies."

The Pony-Mad Princess